PRAISE FOR
LULLABY

"This richly-told tale is haunting and heartbreaking in equal measure. Hazel's story will rip you apart, but her indomitable courage against the oppressive forces in the world will also give you hope. A truly marvelous achievement." —Gwendolyn Kiste, Lambda Literary and Bram Stoker Award-winning author of *Reluctant Immortals* and *The Rust Maidens*

"Exquisitely written and profoundly melancholic, Cécile Guillot's *Lullaby* is a poignant and equally haunting portrait of trauma and injustice that will inevitably linger in the minds of all who are privileged enough to experience this gem of a book." —Eric LaRocca, author of *Things Have Gotten Worse Since We Last Spoke*

"Reminiscent of *The Bell Jar*, *Lullaby* is a gorgeous, gothic fairytale that highlights the very real torment of institutionalized women of the twentieth century. I read it in one sitting!" —Dawn Kurtagich, author of *The Dead House* and *Teeth in the Mist*

"This powerful text, under its apparent poetic caresses, sends you an uppercut to the face. I found this novella perfect, and I really enjoyed the encounter with this author's pen." —Zoé prend la plume

"A moving story in a world that destroys women. A must read!" —Le Punching book

"The writing of Cécile Guillot, delicate and poetic, contributes to this dreamlike and moving bubble that made me shudder more than once. This novella is really perfect for autumn with its disturbing atmosphere of medical experiences, where the limit of reality never ceases to waver." —La lunathèque

LULLABY

CÉCILE GUILLOT

TREPIDATIO
PUBLISHING

ISBN: 978-1-68510-115-2 (sc)
ISBN: 978-1-68510-116-9 (ebook)
Library of Congress Catalog Number: 2023948897

First printing edition: January 5, 2024
Printed by Trepidatio Publishing in the United States of America.
Translated from French by Delphine Roy
Cover Artwork Design: Mikio Murakami
Edited by Sean Leonard
Proofreading, Cover Layout, & Interior Layout by Scarlett R. Algee

Trepidatio Publishing, an imprint of JournalStone Publishing
3205 Sassafras Trail
Carbondale, Illinois 62901

Trepidatio books may be ordered through booksellers or by contacting:
or
JournalStone | www.journalstone.com

My dear, let us enter the abandoned garden

The macabre garden of exquisite wilderness

Where the past roams, alone and fierce,

Like an old king who has lost his crown.

Renée Vivien, "Abandoned Garden"

LULLABY

PROLOGUE

NIGHT WAS CALLING to me in its violet-scented garden of darkness. I was running, my feet among the petals, screaming but silent. Horror had me in its grip, pulling me toward what I wanted to flee, quickly, much too quickly. Because I knew that if I looked, I would go mad. Hidden behind the crumbling, moss-covered wall, I could see him. A dark silhouette over the moonlight. He was still, and at his feet lay a dead body. No, don't look at it. No, no, no.

But my treacherous body wouldn't obey and my eyes grazed the brown curls, the blue lips, the black bruises around the neck. I was looking at my own face, wilting in death. And he started to laugh, mocking my terror and my distress. And as his cruel voice echoed among the green leaves, I was falling, falling...

I switched off the lamp, my heart serene. When stories came to me, I had to lay them down on paper so as not to be haunted by the characters. Night or day, it didn't matter; those vile individuals were as demanding and impatient as spoiled children. I liked that idea. In a sense, I was the mother of my fictional works.

CHAPTER I

EVERY THURSDAY, OUR neighbor, Madame de Martel, and her daughter Blanche came to visit at tea time. We sat together, legs close, taking small sips of the burning drink and nibbling at tiny watercress sandwiches.

"Your *hors d'oeuvres* are delicious," the lady would say in her sing-song accent.

Hors d'oeuvre was a French word I could never properly spell despite my daily lessons. *Ordevre?*

Madame de Martel always brought rose-flavored macaroons, small round treats from her homeland. I impatiently waited for the adults' polished politeness to slip in favor of nasty gossip and tawdry rumor-mongering. That's when Blanche and I were free to go outside in the garden and walk among the flowerbeds. They would shield us from prying eyes. From judgment. There, we could simply be ourselves.

"Summer's ending soon," my friend sighed. "Can you believe I've been here for a year?"

"Do you miss France?" I asked.

She didn't answer, letting her gaze drift over the soft, delicate flowers of the miscanthus bush, twinkling bright in the dying afternoon. I would've liked to keep that image of her forever intact: her beauty and her melancholy, our enchanting surroundings, her blonde hair catching fire in the setting sun like liquid gold.

Then the moment passed. The sun disappeared behind the trees, and darkness settled. The air grew cold, and she shivered.

"Here, take my shawl," I told her as I handed the wool garment to her.

She thanked me with one of her little smiles that filled me with joy. As if it were an honor for me to protect her from the low temperatures of this barbaric country.

I adjusted the shawl on her shoulders and held it in place with a wooden pin. My hand brushed hers. Her skin was so pale and fine. Her name suited her well, just like mine did, I suppose. Hazel, like the tree, except my eyes and hair were a darker shade of brown.

I inhaled quietly to catch a whiff of her lavender perfume. Did she notice? Her eyes met mine and a slight blush colored her cheeks. Embarrassment made a small, trembling laugh escape from my lips.

"Hazel? Blanche?"

I whipped around. My mother was standing at the door of the veranda, glaring at me, her expression unreadable.

"Madame de Martel must go," she added.

We followed her inside. Had she seen something? She wasn't showing a trace of it, but I couldn't meet her eye, and I felt faint for it. As if I'd been caught red-handed, even though I hadn't done anything wrong. Guilt clawed at my heart and wouldn't let go.

*

That evening, as I sat down for supper, my father rose and gave an awkward cough. Something was afoot.

"We've pushed this conversation back far too long. A young lady of your age and status must think about marriage."

The spoon in my hand clattered to the table, clinking against the porcelain plate.

"Marriage?"

"Yes, you heard me. It's high time you found a husband and started a family."

"But I don't want to get married, or have children. At least not for a very long time."

"And what is it you plan on doing in the meantime?" Mother asked in a sharp, sarcastic tone.

Her eyes pinned me. Cold. Calculating.

To be a writer. To publish my horror stories. That's what I wanted to tell them, but I knew it would come off a passing fancy. I couldn't afford to sound childish. I needed to prove that I was mature and reasonable if I wanted them to hear me out. This was undoubtedly serving as my punishment.

"I could be a librarian."

Being surrounded by books all day, that was a good compromise. And a much more pleasant fate than being married off to a stranger. And these days it was a perfectly respectable position for a woman. Nothing and no one would keep me from writing my stories at night.

My mother grasped at her chest. "Working. You're not serious! Why work when a husband can support you?"

I clenched my jaw. We weren't speaking the same language, and we could never understand each other.

"I don't want you to be like those so-called modern women, with their short hair and their harebrained ideas on love and marriage," she went on. "Because when feelings fade, what will they be left with? A marriage of reason means security. And security is what we need as women."

What a terribly boring concept. Coming from her mouth, it sounded like a prison and made me want to flee all the more. To fly in the opposite direction. Danger. Adventure.

But I couldn't act on a whim, so I simply smiled and said, "I don't see myself as a wife and mother. As I told you, I'd rather work and earn my own salary."

My mother shook her head sadly. "I don't understand you. What will people say? They'll think we're too poor to find you a good match."

To be honest, I had never really thought about the future. Adulthood seemed so far away, lost in a fog. As for what other people would say, I didn't give a whit. But the more I thought of it, the more my plan to become a librarian by day and an author by night energized me. As if I'd finally found what I'd been looking for without knowing it.

"Anyway, where would you find a position?" my father argued. "It's ridiculous. You don't know anything about the work force."

"I could go to New York. There must be more positions than here."

"Are you mad?" Mother exclaimed. "New York! A den of sin and danger! A proper woman cannot live there alone. You're raving!"

I didn't point out to her that Father went there on business. It would be useless, just like anything else I could say.

"We've invited James Davidson to dinner tomorrow night. Wait until you've met him before saying you don't want to marry him. And, of course, not a word about your extravagant fantasies," Father added pointedly.

As I left the dining room, I heard him whisper, "Don't worry, she'll come around. She was simply surprised, maybe even frightened. She's still a child, but she'll grow up quickly."

I bit back a joyless laugh. Did I even have the right to an opinion? This is what all those arranged marriages had led to, to consider us women as objects incapable of reason.

I sat at my desk. A cold anger flowed in my veins, and I felt as if my blood was going to slow to a freeze. I couldn't accept the life they were offering me. It would be like being dead. I closed my eyes, trying to imagine a man at my side. His hands on my body. I shook the disturbing image away. I would have to smile and simper and compliment him in front of his business partners and their obedient wives.

I opened my notebook.

Welcome to the masked ball! The monster laughed as champagne flowed. His face was hidden behind silk and feathers, and he could parade in the midst of these humans. Weren't they all impostors, hiding their true nature behind smiles and pretty words? Soon, it would be their blood flowing from the marble fountain...

CHAPTER 2

"DON'T DISAPPOINT ME," my father whispered in my ear.

Even though his tone was low, his words rumbled like thunder, dangerous and threatening. Father could appear to be understanding, but it was only to be more convincing. He had a will of iron, and was a master manipulator.

Mother had chosen my outfit—a yellow dress with jade green trimmings of lace and organza—and had done my hair up in a low chignon, keeping it in place with hair pins that dug into my scalp and made me want to tear at them. I felt like her double. She was wearing a dress of similar colouring and her hair was also tied in a chignon. My hair was naturally wavy, like my father's, but she had straight hair that she had to curl for hours before tying it.

I felt strangely out of place, dressed for a ball when I was just going to attend a boring dinner. Under the veil that replaced actual sleeves, my skin was covered with goosebumps. I would much rather have wrapped my old shawl around my shoulders and sat in front of the fire with a book.

James arrived. I had no doubt met him before at Mother's deadly boring garden parties, but I hadn't paid attention to him. Black hair slicked back, a thin trimmed mustache, drooping brown eyes. A stranger's face, yet he looked like all the other men in my parents' entourage. Even his way of saying hello or pronouncing my name, the corner of his mouth lifting in a small smile, was the same in every way. Did Father only associate with clones? If my mother had any sense of humor, I would have told her so, as she was passionate about gardening.

My father launched into one of his business discussions and I let my mind stray, finding it impossible to listen to a word of this mind-numbing drudgery. I imagined a young girl running away from a sinister manor... I was that girl fleeing in the moonlight, her dress swishing around her with each step.

"I see you find all this quite amusing," James remarked.

"Oh," I said, pulled from my reverie.

Mother frowned at me before taking on a honeyed expression. "Hazel is very interested in the family business. She'll make a fine, devoted wife, an incomparable support for whoever is lucky enough to marry her."

"Really?"

I couldn't hold back my laughter. My parents froze in their seats, glaring daggers at me, while my suitor gaped at me, flabbergasted.

"I'm sorry," I said. "I don't like hypocrisy. I must admit that all this business stuff confounds me."

"I understand. These are men's concerns. It must all seem quite complicated to you."

His comment was like a douse of cold water. "Are you implying that women aren't smart enough to deal with these questions?" I asked in a falsely innocent tone.

"Of course. It's been proven. Thankfully you have other talents."

I burst out laughing. "Other talents? Like procreation, you mean? How regrettable to be so narrow-minded. Women—"

I was unable to finish my sentence. My father slammed his fist on the table, his face red with fury.

"That's enough from you this evening. We'll hear no more of your comments. James, please excuse my daughter's insolence."

The atmosphere weighed down on the table like lead. My father and his guest tried to talk about politics and the economy, but their conversation was forced, their words only attempting to fill the awkward silence.

*

The evening had been disastrous, but I was somehow relieved. I hoped my parents would now understand that I wasn't fit to be married off and would leave me alone.

I lay in bed and closed my eyes. Behind my eyelids, I could see a monster prowling among the ivy, waiting his turn. I pushed the vision back, too exhausted to let my imagination stray or to write. I just wanted to think about Blanche and the way her hair caught fire in the setting sun.

CHAPTER 3

IT WAS THURSDAY, and I was impatient to see Blanche and tell her about the other evening's dismal dinner. I was certain she would also find James terribly boring and get a good laugh out of my misadventures. However, as time ticked by, there was no sign of Madame de Martel.

"Isn't our neighbor coming for tea today?" I asked, worried.

"No, not this week," my mother answered tersely. "Nor any other week for that matter. She's preparing to go back to France."

"What? Why didn't you tell me anything?" I exclaimed. "When are they leaving? I have to say goodbye to Blanche."

The idea of never seeing my dear friend again seized my heart and I gripped the damask armchair, certain that I would collapse if I let go. My mother noticed my distress and turned away, her lips pinched.

"We don't have time to receive them today. The seamstress will be here soon, I ordered new dresses for you. You must be perfect for the coming soirées. There should be a lot more than usual," she sighed.

To find a husband, I told myself. They hadn't been deterred by our discussion at dinner from going ahead with their plan. If I hadn't felt so sad, I would have been angry at being considered a pretty bauble to be given away. A bit of lace, a few ribbons, and there's a gift, all ready to be used in a commercial exchange.

I went to the parlor, dragging my feet but forcing myself to smile when I saw Miss Carmody, her measuring tape around her neck. She had always been kind to me and was in no way responsible for my situation. Nonetheless, her compassionate expression told me that my smile looked more like a grimace.

"Hello, my dear child— What am I saying, you're a young lady now. How could you grow up so fast?"

"Hello," I murmured.

She had dressed me since childhood and her soft manners were like a balm for my poor saddened heart. She had always treated me with more warmth than my own mother.

"I'm going to have to take your measurements again. It looks like you've filled out. Do you have any ideas on colors or materials?" she asked, watching me with her piercing eyes.

I shrugged. It was of no interest to me. I couldn't stop thinking about Blanche, and how I might never see her again. Then, suddenly, I thought about the embroidered ribbon she had given me once.

"Wait here, I have something I'd like to use."

Her face brightened up when faced with my newfound enthusiasm. My idea was perfect. I could keep a little piece of Blanche close to my heart. Maybe I could find a way to slip out before she left and give her a small keepsake so she wouldn't forget me.

Lost in thought, I opened the door to my room. My mother was standing there, livid, my notebook in hand. Horror struck me. For a moment, I was unable to breathe. All my stories were there, at her mercy.

"No," I sobbed.

I launched myself at her to tear the notebook from her hands so that she couldn't read another word. But my fate was already sealed. I knew as soon as our eyes met; before she tripped backward and knocked the back of her skull against the dressing table. My momentum had caused me to shove my mother, and I found myself on the floor, hugging my precious child against my breast, as footsteps thundered in the hallway. I could no longer breathe, I wanted time to stop, so I closed my eyes, hanging onto my notebook like a lifebuoy.

CHAPTER 4

AFTER BEING LOCKED up in my room for five days, I was finally told I could come out and that I was expected in the living room.

I went down the steps as slowly as a convict in no hurry to meet their executioner.

I was surprised to see that my parents weren't alone. Standing beside them was a tall man with thick, curly hair.

"You probably don't remember your uncle George. We invited him here to ask for advice where you're concerned. He's a doctor," my father explained.

"My brother hasn't visited in so long," my mother said. "If only we had been reunited under less dire circumstances."

Dire. It was as if she was talking about a funeral. Mine, according to my mother's grief-stricken expression.

I couldn't bring myself to meet my uncle's eye, and I kept my head down.

"I thought it was your diary. Your friendship with that Blanche girl seemed suspect to me... But I couldn't imagine uncovering such horrors," my mother went on, dabbing the corner of her eyes with her handkerchief. "You have a perverse mind. To think such a monster lived in my household for all these years. Thank goodness you're here to help, my dear George."

A monster. The term was like a punch to the gut. Did she really see me that way? Was she right? Cold sweat trickled down my spine. She started to sob and her brother patted her shoulder.

"I know the perfect place," he said. "She can be cured. Don't worry. She'll come back with a pure, blank mind."

A stone settled in my stomach. No doubt because they were about me as if I wasn't here, but mostly because they were talking of sending me away. I had imagined a flood of disapproval. Vile accusations. Harsh, cutting words. But not that.

Where did they plan on taking me? For how long? What would be done to me? Could one extract a rotten soul like one would a decayed tooth? I was starting to worry. I was about to start asking questions, but my father cut me short.

"There's nothing you can say. Not after what you did. Go and pack, your uncle will drive you there."

So I was to leave immediately? Panic swept through me, taking everything in its wake, and I started to cry pitifully. I was afraid, for not only had I lost the meager affection of my parents, but I also had no idea what was to become of me. I wanted to throw myself at their feet, beg for forgiveness, promise that I would change... But was that even possible? It would be like trying to stop breathing. Reason seemed to have left me; I couldn't think anymore, my thoughts swirling in my mind.

I was angry at myself for such a display of vulnerability when I was usually capable of self-control, but the idea of *a pure, blank mind* kept echoing in my head. Faced with my father's obvious exasperation, I fled to my room, where no one could see my tears, and started to pack a few belongings. Taking one object, then another, before putting them back, undecided. I didn't know what I was supposed to bring with me. How can you choose when you don't know if the trip will last a day, a week, a month, a year...or longer?

I had thought myself a sensible, reasonable person, almost an adult, but I was nothing but a terrified child. I had never left the house, not even for a holiday. I had once dreamed of filling that new, useless suitcase to go on an adventure in New York. It all seemed so foolish now.

I opened my suitcase and packed a few nightgowns, day dresses, underclothes, and brushes. I added Blanche's ribbon, a blank notebook—my mother having kept the one that held my stories—and a small volume of French poetry that my friend had given me. She had translated the verses into English in the margin, in her neat cursive writing.

When you came, thoughtfully, into the mist
The sky melded gold with crystal and bronze.
Your body was a wisp, a vague undulation,
Suppler and fresher than a foamy wave.
The summer night seemed an oriental dream
Of rose and sandalwood.

I closed my eyes, holding the book to my heart. Hoping it would give me courage.

Then I went down into the entrance hall, put a light shawl around my shoulders, and waited in silence. My uncle joined me quickly, bringing with him a smell of tobacco that made me sick to my stomach. He opened the door without a look in my direction, as if I was nothing but a parcel to be delivered.

At the foot of the stairs, I glanced back at the house that was supposed to be my home. No one came out. No one stood at the window. So, my parents didn't even plan on saying goodbye? Didn't I deserve the bare minimum of social graces?

I followed my uncle down the gravel path, like a puppet devoid of will, a broken doll. The late August sky was a perfect, cloudless blue. Birds sang in the trees. The air was still a bit cool, but soon the sun would shine bright and hot, and my mother would go tend to her flowers.

I climbed in his shiny, probably brand-new Ford T and closed my eyes. I wasn't in the mood to look at a pretty summer landscape. Behind my eyelids, my monster seemed to taunt me. Challenging me to write a story. But my thoughts were muddied. *A garden at night, where time stood still.* The words rolled over my tongue and I savored them like candy. Maybe it was just an escape. Or an idea my muse was whispering to me, that would eventually become a story in the next few weeks.

After several minutes, or perhaps several hours, the car stopped, pulling me from my daydream. My uncle opened the passenger door and I finally met his gaze. Cold and hard, and I was irrationally reminded of a snake. I held my shawl tighter, pretending to be chilled by the cool wind. I didn't want to show my weaknesses. With what I hope was a dignified air, I crossed the alley lined with white dahlias, probably the last of the season.

In front of me stood an austere red brick building with large windows. It looked like an angry red face staring at me with dark eyes. Judging me. I shook my head. What a silly idea. I had to get ahold of myself.

But my will faltered when a nurse opened the door. Doubts assailed me. What were they going to do to me?

I followed the nurse and my uncle down a long corridor covered in gold-framed mirrors. A terrified, doe-eyed Hazel stared back at me, a strange vision that made my head spin. My heart was beating so hard I felt as if the noise was echoing off the walls for everyone to hear.

We arrived in a large room where, I was told, the patients could gather or receive visitors. It looked like a fancy tea shop, but the looming presence of a giant of a man didn't leave any doubt as to where we were. The ivory and gold damask walls, the delicate cream curtains, the potted plants; everything was so elegant. I was almost surprised. However, nothing lay on the tables or the shelves. No object that could be broken or thrown. Were they afraid we would assault someone with a Faberge egg?

The idea might have made me smile if the horror of my situation wasn't creeping up on me. I was being interned in an insane asylum. I let out a whimper and my uncle frowned. I immediately cast my eyes down, staring at the toes of my shoes.

"Here's your new patient, Hazel Bloom. Everything has been settled with Doctor Pierce."

"Yes, we've been expecting you."

"Good. My work here is done then."

He left me there with a vague goodbye, as if he'd come back within the hour. As if he wasn't locking me up, perhaps forever, in an insane asylum.

CHAPTER 5

I FOLLOWED THE nurse into a much more austere corridor. She took me to a small room and declared, "You can keep your dress, but you have to take off your jewelry and your hairpins. Your belongings will be kept in a safe."

I took out my hairpins and heavy locks of hair tumbled down my back. I rummaged through my things and took out Blanche's precious gift. I braided my hair and tied it with the ribbon.

"Follow me. I'll show you to your room."

In the corridor, a woman was writhing on the ground, arching as growls tore from her throat. I looked at the nurse, alarmed, but she ignored the woman. Was such a spectacle common around here? Probably. A bit further, a young girl stared into space and hummed, half her face hidden behind long pale hair.

I arrived in my room at last. The furniture was sparse: a bed with a porcelain chamber pot, a nightstand, a lamp, a chest of drawers, and a small desk.

"Here's the schedule," the nurse said in a flat tone. "Up at eight, breakfast at eight thirty, art class at nine thirty, free time at eleven— you can read or play checkers—lunch at noon, walk in the gardens at one, and therapy with Doctor Bromfield at two. At four, there's choir, and dinner is served at six. Lights out at nine o'clock."

"That's a...busy schedule," I remarked, surprised by the number of activities.

"A busy mind is a healthy mind. We can't let our patients give in to inappropriate thoughts. Idleness is the mother of all sin," she added as if she was reciting a well-honed lesson. "It's five past eleven, I'll let you return to the living area."

The two women we'd passed in the corridor weren't there anymore. In the room with the damask walls, two elderly patients were playing checkers, while an adolescent traced her finger along the pattern of the tapestry, hypnotized. A fourth patient, a young woman, was sitting at the table in front of an open book.

She looked up and gave me a slight smile. I walked over to her, as she was a beacon in the storm. I was so lost that the smallest sign of friendliness was a welcome sight.

"Glad to meet the newest patient of Montrose Asylum," she said in a solemn tone. "I'm Josephine Foley, but I go by Jo."

"Hazel Bloom," I replied in a wavering tone.

Josephine had short wavy black hair. The type of fashionable hairstyle that my mother hated. One could tell her hair had been shorter but had grown out a bit. She looked at me, or rather looked me over, with eyes as green and cold as jade. She seemed awfully contemptuous, and I almost regretted having walked up to her. But who else could I turn to? Her pointed face was delicate and beautiful, but an intimidating sort of beauty. She must have been around twenty, but her aura of confidence was such that she looked mature and worldly. How could I have thought she'd be friendly?

And what could she be doing here? She seemed much more lucid than the other young women I'd seen since arriving.

"So, why did they lock you up?"

I hadn't been expecting such a direct question. I was trying to read her, not understanding why she was acting this way, forthright and arrogant at the same time. I dug my fingernails into my palms, as if the pain could tether me.

"I write stories," I stammered, trying to get ahold of myself.

"Stories," she repeated, raising an eyebrow. "And what's so special about these stories?"

"They're a bit bloody."

She burst out laughing, then added, "I'm not making fun, at least not of you. I don't know why men fear us so much that they have to imprison us." Her gaze softened, her expression now almost playful. "I think you and I will get along."

"What about you? Why are you here?"

She looked at me for a moment in silence. "I suppose I can tell you. I was arrested while I was demonstrating with my comrades of the NWP."

"The what?"

"The National Woman's Party. It's an organization of people demanding rights. Like equality between men and women in the workplace. It's thanks to them that we can vote."

I felt so stupid. My family was so closed off from the world. Mother hated modernity, which she considered immoral, and seldom talked about politics. As for Father, he was more interested in business.

"Do you think it's normal that we're paid less? That we're not allowed to do certain jobs?"

"I admit I never thought of it."

"We're not less intelligent than men; on the contrary," she stated, lifting her chin.

I could only nod. These last few days had proven to me how right she was. We women were treated as inferior beings, incapable of choosing our own destiny.

"Not long ago, I met a woman, Margaret," she went on. "She was talking about medical ways to prevent pregnancy, easily accessible to all girls. She was arrested and almost ended up in jail. She had to flee to Europe for more than a year, but that didn't stop her. She founded the American Birth Control League and distributed a pamphlet for young ladies. We need more women like her. Women who aren't afraid to express themselves!"

She ended her sentence by thumping her fist on the table. She glanced at the nurse, then straightened herself and forced her expression to be more neutral.

"Here, in any case, it's better to abstain."

"Abstain?"

"From expressing ourselves. We have to pretend to be sweet and docile. Which doctor is treating you?"

"Doctor Bromfield."

"Good. He's harmless. He believes in the healing power of words. Whatever you do, don't confide in him. Tell him what he wants to hear and you'll be free soon."

"And what's that?"

"That your sessions have enlightened your mind. But wait a few days, or he won't believe you."

"And how long have you been here?"

"Too long, I admit. I got off to a rough start, but hydrotherapy taught me a valuable lesson."

"Hydro—"

I was interrupted by the nurse who was ringing the bell for lunchtime. I didn't know if this conversation should reassure me or alarm me. Everything here was so strange.

*

Later, it was time for a walk. I thought that being outdoors would do me good, but once I was in the gardens of the hospital, I didn't know what to do with myself. I stood there, hesitant, on the gravel path, staring at the well-trimmed hedges. The other patients were already sitting in the shade of the large elm.

Jo joined me and started telling me everyone's name. "See over there, the two old ladies, that's Mary and Helen. They've been here for thirty years. Mary has epilepsy, and Helen's husband had her committed because she went mad after her child was stillborn."

"That's terrible. But aren't they cured? They seem to be doing well."

"I guess it's easier for some of them to stay here instead of going out into the world again." I didn't know if her words were a simple statement or a reproach. "And over there, the redhead, she's hysterical. She often throws fits, it's something to see."

"Yes, I saw that when I arrived. What about the young girl?"

"Ann. She's only fourteen. They say she never talked. She never looks anyone in the eye. It's like we don't exist for her."

I let my gaze roam over the lawn. "Aren't there people missing?"

"Yes, some people have long and tiring treatments."

She pinched her lips in displeasure. I felt like I had an ally, but a strange one, truth be told. She was so cold and proud, and yet she wasn't loathe to give me advice.

The nurse clapped her hands so the walk could begin. We lined up obediently and started to walk on the gravel path that wound across the gardens. Little by little, the whispers and giggles faded away and a gloomy atmosphere descended over us.

"Every day we walk down the same path, it's so boring," Jo remarked. "They think physical exercise is good for our nerves, and I suppose it's better than being locked up all day. It's enough to go crazy!"

She winked at me and smiled. I stifled a laugh. I didn't expect the proud Josephine Foley to make a joke.

The time for my therapy with Doctor Bromfield had come fast. I was nervous, but Jo had reassured me a little. At least I was going to get the most harmless of treatments.

The nurse knocked on the door and opened it. A middle-aged man was sitting at his desk, scribbling notes on a piece of paper. He rifled through a stack of files, then took out an envelope as he signaled for me to sit down in the chair in front of him.

"Miss Bloom. I will be your doctor while you stay here. I have your uncle's letter here, I see he's a doctor as well. You have written morbid and unwholesome things, and hit your mother. Your parents fear you have unnatural inclinations."

I wanted to object, to explain that I hit my mother by accident, but it would have only emphasized the fact that I had indeed written horror stories, or that I liked girls. Where was the harm in that? Had they locked Mary Shelley up for writing *Frankenstein*? Or Renée Vivien for writing poetry to her lover? However, I thought back on what Jo had said and decided to stay quiet. I looked down demurely and waited for the rest.

"I want to emulate my European colleagues, and I'm convinced that words have the power to heal. The important thing is to be sincere and honest. Don't be afraid to tell me what you feel."

"All right," I said in a small voice, keeping my eyes fixed on the Bakelite clock on the shelf.

"So, how are you feeling today?"

I searched my mind for a harmless answer that would keep me out of danger. That would sound normal.

"Everything is so new. But I hope with all my heart that I'll recover and go back to my family."

I nearly winced when I said the word "recover." As if I were sick...

"We're going to purify your mind from these vices that are tormenting you."

Tormenting me? They're what make me happy, I wanted to say. The only thing that had tormented me these past weeks was the way my parents looked at me. A monster. The word was digging into my heart like a thorn. Was my mother right?

"But how?" I couldn't help but ask out of despair and curiosity. How could speaking have any consequence on how someone behaved?

"By facing what you are. Search within yourself for what's hidden and bring it up to the light. Don't be afraid."

All this sounded very vague, but I preferred this to the infamous hydrotherapy.

That night, I lay in bed, exhausted. It wasn't so much the suggested activities, which were all boring, that had tired me out, but the tension I had accumulated. The confrontation with my parents, my arrival in this awful place, the unknown and uncertainty about the future...

Despite all of this, sleep eluded me. I tossed and turned, but the mattress was too hard for me to find a comfortable position. I pushed the cover back then pulled it up again a few minutes later. And I could see the light coming under the door from the corridor, as it was always on. In this sepulchral silence, the oddity of my situation was only more disconcerting.

I had never slept anywhere else other than my own room, in my house. What if I couldn't sleep in an unfamiliar environment? Would I simply have sleepless night after sleepless night? Would I not wilt away and die being uprooted this way?

CHAPTER 6

I GOT UP the next morning with a heavy sensation that made my feet drag. I hadn't slept and my tired brain was starting to imagine bizarre stories I had to write down on paper.

An abandoned garden where everything dies...

I got dressed, my mind in a fog, filled with a multitude of dark fantasies.

An abandoned garden where souls dance under the moonlight under the pleased eye of the beast...

"Hurry up and go take your breakfast," a nurse admonished me. "Here we don't tolerate laziness. Maybe you were used to lolling around and taking breakfast in bed, but that's over now!"

It wasn't the same person as the previous day. This one was older and much less pleasant.

"Sorry, I haven't been able to sleep."

I rubbed my eyes to get rid of the impression that stones were weighing my lashes down.

"I'll tell the doctor to prescribe you some bromine."

I followed her to the dining room where everyone was already seated. Jo had saved a seat for me next to her, unless the empty chair was only a coincidence or due to her peculiar personality.

The nurse set a platter in front of me with half a grapefruit, fried eggs, bacon, a fish cake, and a cup of coffee. My stomach lurched at the smell. In front of me, two eyes observed me keenly.

"I'm Gloria."

"Hello, I'm Hazel."

"I know. You don't look hungry."

Jo nudged me with her elbow.

"You want some?" I asked hesitantly.

"Oh! So nice of you to offer!"

Gloria grabbed the cake and stuffed it in an already full pocket, then tipped the bacon and eggs onto her plate.

"Rough night?" Jo asked.

"Yes," I admitted.

"You'll get used to it."

An abandoned garden...

"Tell me," I implored her. "Where can I find something to write with? Should I ask the nurse? The one who was there this morning doesn't seem very nice."

"Write? You can forget about it. It's forbidden."

"What?"

How would I write my stories? The ones throbbing in my brain, threatening to make my head explode?

The reality of my situation suddenly hit me. I was here because of what I'd written. Even if writing had been allowed, no one would give me anything that could enable my vices.

"As for Bertha, she's not nice at all. I prefer Mabel by a mile. Beware of her, she hates us and thinks we're spoiled."

"Spoiled? Even if we're locked up?"

"At least we have food and warm clothes for winter... I heard about the conditions in the asylums for poor women."

She shivered and brought her cup of coffee to her lips.

"So you really think we're...lucky?"

"No, I just think our conditions could be worse. Some therapies are inhumane, no matter if we're rich or poor. In that respect, there's no difference."

"Like hydrotherapy?"

I waited for her to go on, to tell me what she'd experienced, but she simply nodded. Jo liked to talk, but she wasn't inclined to reveal anything intimate about herself.

"Miss Foley, you have your monthly interview with Doctor Pierce," Bertha announced.

"Sorry, I have to go. Oh, and another thing! For the art session, don't use too much black if you don't want Bromfield on your case."

I opened my mouth to reply, but she was already gone. I was going to have to go to the art workshop alone.

"Can I stay with you, Gloria?" I asked pitifully.

"Oh, my stomach hurts, I'm going to go to the bathroom," she replied, holding her stomach.

"Gloria Havisham, you've stolen food from your friends again! You can be sure we'll tell Doctor Pierce," Bertha barked.

I went alone to the workshop, falling in line with the patients who were walking slowly down the corridor. I had already had art lessons. Generally, the professor gave us a model—a bouquet of flowers or a basket of fruit—and we had to reproduce it identically, taking care of the shades and the colors. Nothing like that here. Everyone just haphazardly applied paint on the white paper, spreading it as much as possible. I looked at the young girl with pale blonde hair, the one I'd seen when I arrived. She had already blackened her paper and was starting to paint a red spot in the middle.

"That's very...interesting. What is it?"

She looked up at me and shrugged her shoulder before grabbing the paper and stuffing it in the trash can.

"Sorry, I didn't mean to offend you."

She went to sit in the back of the room. I wanted to follow her, but the nurse's angry voice dissuaded me.

"Please get to work, Miss Bloom."

*

The worst part of the day was the free time. Despite the presence of the other patients, I felt terribly alone. Lost. I walked to the row of books. Alas, I realized that the choice was limited: Bibles and more Bibles. And a few copies of *Guide to Becoming a Suitable Young Woman*, written by Doctor Pierce himself. I took a copy and sat down.

"Don't bother! Our dear old doctor thinks a woman is only good for serving her husband and providing him with healthy heirs."

Josephine was back! Relief swept through me. She was my only landmark in this strange place filled with strange, hostile faces.

CHAPTER 7

THE DAY HAD been exhausting. How many more would this masquerade last? I was happy to have met Jo, despite her peculiar character, for without her presence, time would have gone by much more slowly and dully. And anguish would have no doubt suffocated me.

I fell asleep as soon as I lay down on the bed. The medicine the nurse had given me earlier probably helped.

Something suddenly woke me up. I didn't know if I'd been asleep a few minutes or a few hours. I got up and walked to the corridor. Bizarrely, it was dark and empty. A few doors down, Jo's door opened. She stuck out her head and shot me a questioning look. We could hear faint music, and listening carefully, one could make out a child's voice. It was a lullaby.

Jo left her room and I joined her.

She took my hand and we followed the melody, like the children of Hamelin walking toward their gruesome fate. With every step, the words grew clearer.

My darling doll
Will not sleep
Close your pretty eyes
Your sapphire eyes
Golden angel
How you pain me
Sleep, little doll, sleep, sleep
Or I shall die

I couldn't help but shudder. In front of us, there was a door.

"Where are we?" I whispered.

"Behind that, there's just a corridor and rooms that are out of use. No one goes there. It's empty and cold."

How did she know? She wasn't the type to let herself be stopped by a "No Entry" sign. Maybe she even took pleasure purposely breaking the rules. I felt torn between two opposite feelings: the pressing need to follow the voice and understand what was happening, and the desire to flee as far away as possible from this place. The song was like a siren's call for me, bewitching and fatal.

"What's going on?"

I startled and turned around toward the person who'd just spoken. A few steps away stood the young woman I'd seen when I arrived, then during painting class. The one with the long blonde hair. Her eyes were foggy with sleep and her voice raspy. She, too, had been awoken by the strange melody.

"Lulla Davis," Josephine said as if she was introducing us.

The lullaby stopped. But it only made me want to open that door all the more to see what it was hiding. Could a child be there? Perhaps one of the night nurse's daughters? Jo stepped up and pushed the door open. The corridor lay before us, dark and menacing. Light, musical laughter rang out and the voice seemed to grow more distant, urging us to follow it, but neither of us moved. A slight movement caught my eye. It was a moth with golden wings. I stood there watching it, not knowing how to react. The situation seemed unreal. Was I dreaming?

Jo stepped back and collided into me, pulling me out of my thoughts. I looked up. She was staring at something. A moving shadow in the darkness.

"There's something there," she whispered.

We heard a rustling sound. Leaves? Whatever it was, it couldn't be good. I turned around, ready to run.

Lulla was staring at me, her hand against her chest, eyes wide. She, too, seemed to have seen something, but I didn't have time to ask her. I grasped her elbow and pulled her along. It shocked her awake and she started to run next to me. I could hear Josephine's steps behind us.

When we arrived in our corridor, we finally stopped to catch our breath.

"This is crazy," Jo panted.

"We're in an asylum," I said, vying for a joke.

"All of this is so strange. I hope we didn't wake the night nurse. We'd better go to sleep. Maybe it'll all seem clearer in the morning," she concluded before slipping back to her room, her expression still troubled.

I turned to Lulla. She stood there in the middle of the corridor, trembling.

"You should go to bed too."

She nodded, but I could tell she was lost.

"Did you see...?"

I didn't finish my sentence. No need. She knew what I meant.

"No."

"Come on," I said, holding out my hand to take her back to her room.

She stepped back in horror. And a hint of fear.

That's when I saw it. Her hand. Or rather, the fact that she had none to speak of. Her arm ended in a sort of twisted growth. So that's what she had been hiding—and during the painting class too.

I wanted to say sorry, but the girl whipped around and ran away. I followed her, not knowing what I was going to do. I had to make amends, but she slammed the door in my face, leaving me alone with my guilt and my shame.

*

The next day, I went to see Lulla before breakfast. I could tell she was embarrassed. She slipped on a nightgown with long sleeves that hid her misshapen hand. To see her so thin and fragile and broken gripped my heart.

"You don't have to be ashamed," I said.

She looked away so I wouldn't see her eyes brimming with tears. "Leave me alone. I have to go. It's almost time for my treatment."

Indeed, a nurse arrived to take her away. I went to the dining room, distressed. I wanted to be useful, but Lulla didn't want my help.

"Why the long face?" Jo asked, sitting beside me.

"I tried to go talk to Lulla..."

"I see. Don't take it personally, she's the same with everyone. She's been here so long..."

"I just wanted to help her."

"That's very generous of you, but if it were that simple, she wouldn't be locked up in here."

"I suppose," I muttered. "What is this treatment anyway?"

"A rebirth," Jo answered sarcastically.

"Pardon?"

"I overheard the doctors talking about it several times. Something about an insulin shock—don't ask me what that means. But when the patient wakes up, it's a veritable rebirth for her. I can't tell you how many times I've seen Lulla be born, or come back to life; I don't know what you should call it. And I've only been here a few months."

"But that's horrible!"

"That's why it's better to talk to Doctor Bromfield. Talking is harmless, especially if you tell him what he wants to hear."

"I thought you had to be sincere to get well again."

"Get well from what? We don't need to get well, we need to get out of here. Believe me, better Bromfield than Pierce. If he could cut us up to do his experiments, he would."

I shuddered at her words.

"May you never enter that man's study... On the wall, there's a framed quote. And we're the crazy ones?"

"A quote?"

"Yes." She closed her eyes to recite it. "The garden of humanity is very full of weeds. Nurture will never transform them into flowers."

I stared at her, confused, not knowing what to say.

"That means," she explained, faced with my silence, "that degenerates like us will never get better. Or worse, if we have children, they'll inherit our flaws."

"That's pessimistic. Depressing, even."

"It's worse, actually. Some patients like Mary were operated on. Sterilized. I heard things. They're waiting for little Ann to turn sixteen."

"That's horrible!"

Such actions seemed barbarian to me. I trembled just to think of it. It was worse than I had imagined coming here. I really needed to find a way to get out. True, I didn't want children, but I didn't want anyone cutting me up either. Splitting my stomach open to extract whichever organ they needed.

"How do you know so many things?"

"I lie low, I shuffle around, and I listen... Knowledge is power! If my arrival hadn't been so eventful, I would already be gone. I have to be twice as smart because of the ruckus I caused. And twice as patient. Don't do as I did, keep your head down. If all goes well, I'll be out of here in a month."

I wanted to talk about the previous evening, but I didn't find the courage to do so. The whole thing seemed nothing else than a bad dream in broad daylight. Our imaginations must have gotten carried away in the night.

*

It was time for my second interview with Bromfield. If he wanted me to be sincere, that's just what I was going to do, and hopefully it would pay. After all, where was the harm in asking for a few books?

"Everything is fine, Doctor, but I'm a bit sad."

"Really?"

"Yes, I realized we don't have a lot of choice when it comes to reading. I know my Bible by heart and I would have liked some poetry to brighten my days."

I carefully omitted the volume already in my possession.

"You're here to get better. Too much reading is bad for the female mind. You see, female cells are analogical, destined to conserve energy and sustain life. Whereas male cells are catabolical, geared toward action. Excessive reading may thus slow your recovery, or even hinder it altogether."

I hadn't understood a word he'd said, but I knew I wouldn't prevail. How could one live without reading and writing?

A storm of distress and anger was rising within me. It was as if I was being stripped of any reason to live. Locked up without paper or pen, with marriage as my only redemption. No. A thousand times no.

But I swallowed back the bitter taste that flooded my mouth and put honey on my words.

"Oh! I understand. I'm happy to talk to you, Doctor. You make everything so much clearer. I'm sure I'll recover. You give me hope."

In my head, words were screaming, demanding to be let out on paper... *An abandoned garden... A fountain of blood... A scent of nightshade... A beating crimson heart... A shroud of dreams...*

*

When I told Jo about the session, she reacted with glee.

"Wonderful! That doctor is so naïve. I wish I had been as crafty as you from the start, then maybe I'd be free..."

I didn't reply, selfishly thinking that if she hadn't been there, locked up with me, I would have been lost. To face all of this alone, without her, seemed impossible to me. Faced with my silence, she sank deep in thought. Her face hardened and her eyes grew steely with determination, her hands curled so tight her knuckles were white.

"I'm not a pretty bouquet of flowers that one places on the mantelpiece then leaves to wilt. I'm a poisonous flower. A dangerous one. Try to eat her and she will kill you. I won't let myself be governed by any man, least of all my husband. I need to get out and take back the reins."

CHAPTER 8

MY DARLING DOLL
  Will not sleep
  Close your pretty eyes
  Your sapphire eyes
  Golden angel
  How you pain me
  Sleep, little doll, sleep, sleep
  Or I shall die

I looked at Jo and saw in her eyes the same determination that burned within me. This was real, and this time, we wouldn't flee. We would uncover the mystery of the child and her lullaby. Or so I hoped. Deep inside, I needed to know, to understand. I took her hand and stepped forward. The door leading to the corridor opened on its own, slowly. We took a step. We were in an alley covered with ivy. I could see a little girl running far ahead and disappearing in the darkness. Moths fluttered around us. One of them landed on my arm. I felt a hand slip into mine. It was Lulla.

She was evanescent, magnificent. As beautiful and luminous as Blanche; but if Blanche was like the sun, Lulla was the moon. Hair so pale one couldn't determine if it was blonde, white, or gray, and eyes like marbles reflecting a heavenly body. Her presence overwhelmed, and knowing that she had spent most of her life between the walls of Montrose Asylum revolted me. I wanted to be the one to rescue her, but I was a prisoner all the same.

I smiled at her, glad for her presence at our side and relieved that she wasn't holding my clumsiness against me. The three of us marched forward, holding onto each other. The song had stopped, and as we made our way through the garden, the leaves started to take on a golden russet hue.

"It's already fall here," whispered Lulla.

Purple meadow saffrons swayed in the wind, though we could not feel it ourselves. Twilight bathed the garden in a pale, silvery hue. I looked around. The corridor was gone, and there was nothing but this enchanting landscape.

"It's stunning," Lulla said.

And I saw in her gaze that all was forgiven.

"Impossible," Jo replied. "A corridor can't transform itself into a garden. Here, it's fall already. We're not even in September."

"Are we dreaming?" I murmured, not knowing what to think.

I stroked my naked arm. There were goosebumps on my skin. Maybe it wasn't a dream after all.

"No matter," Lulla said. "It's so beautiful here... We can rest. Be who we want."

What a tempting idea.

Lulla started to dance among the flowers, her white nightgown floating around her ankles.

"Come on," she urged me.

I took her hand and joined her in her whimsical dance until my head spun. We fell together in the lush green grass. I felt like I hadn't laughed in months, centuries. The burden that had been weighing down on me since my notebook had been discovered slowly lifted, leaving me feeling light-headed and euphoric. I remained in the grass and admired the butterflies, their iridescent golden green wings, their hypnotic ballet in the opal light. And the sensation of Lulla's skin against mine, our entwined fingers.

Jo cleared her throat, ending my reverie. She helped us up and nodded toward something, frowning. I looked over and saw the little girl, half hidden behind a tree trunk. I took a step toward her but she ran away with a giggle. Was she asking us to follow her in the shade of the foliage? Jo placed a hand on my shoulder and held me back.

"We don't know what this place is," she warned. "We should stay on our guard."

Lulla held her misshapen hand to her heart, waiting for a verdict.

"Maybe..."

Josephine never finished her sentence. The ground started to shake beneath our feet. The leaves rustled and a slight moan rose from the greenery.

Something was slowly approaching. Something massive. With each step, the flowers trembled and the grass shivered against my ankles. The earth shuddered with each movement of this hungry, impatient creature.

Jo didn't wait for the creature, whatever it was, to arrive in the garden. She grabbed my arm and pulled. Lulla was running beside us, her long hair floating behind her in the silvery light. She looked like a fairy. A dream. A nightmare.

The corridor seemed to stretch on forever, and as we ran, furious steps rumbled against the ground. Were we being chased? I didn't dare look behind me to find out. Would the monster catch us? Blood pulsed in my ears, and I couldn't tell whether the roar I heard came from my heart or our assailant.

The door appeared at last and Jo slammed it open, still pulling me behind her. We were back in the real world. Could the creature follow us here?

"What's the meaning of all this commotion?" thundered Bertha.

I froze a few feet away from my room. Jo was breathless and speechless, for once. And where was Lulla? In our haste, we had lost her. Had she gone back to bed, or was she hiding in the corridor? Unless she had remained stuck in the magical garden. I looked around in a panic. What if the monster had caught her? I needed to find her.

Alas, before I could ask myself any more questions, a needle pricked my arm and I sank into darkness.

CHAPTER 9

I WOKE UP the next morning with a headache and a vague sensation of nausea. My body was heavy, but I managed to get out of bed. It was already daylight and the sun pierced through the curtains. Why had I slept for so long? Little by little, memories of the previous night came back to me. The garden. Lulla. The menacing presence. The nurse. I rubbed my temples to alleviate my migraine.

The corridor and the living room were empty. It must have been time for our walk. I looked outside, searching for my friends, but there was no one in sight.

I went back. Lulla was sleeping in her bed, rigid under her white cover like a recumbent statue. I closed the door again so as not to wake her and Josephine joined me.

"Hard time waking up, huh?"

"A bit," I replied. "Lulla's still sleeping."

She grimaced and placed a hand on her forehead. "They could have knocked out a horse with such a dose of tranquilizer!"

I nodded, my mind too foggy to elaborate a response. The light burned my eyes, and I felt like every inch of my body had been beaten. Was this what was in store for me whenever I misbehaved? Every day I discovered a new form of torture. I remembered Bertha's smug smirk when she'd plunged the needle into my flesh. I really had to find a way to flee from this place and these evil people.

I hesitated, then asked, "Have you already thought about what you'll do when you're free?"

"Free? What an apt choice of words. Yes, I think about it every day. I'm going to ask for a divorce. My parents own a house not far from New York, I'll go live there. I can more easily dedicate myself to the female cause there, people are less narrow-minded than in small towns. And in the evening I'll go dance the Charleston and drink Jack Roses while listening to jazz."

I realized the extent of my family's petty existence, refusing modernity and change, forever stuck in outdated values. An existence where women don't work, don't choose who they marry, and don't write books, unless they're love stories.

"What about you?" she asked.

"I don't know. I'd like to write novels. I thought I could find work in a library. But after all you've been through, don't you regret your choices? Are you going to start up again?"

"Of course. The only thing I regret is having agreed to this sham of a marriage. Alfred is the worst sort of boor. He's the one who locked me up here. I'm not good for his image in the eyes of voters."

"He's a politician then?"

"Only in his dreams. He never got enough votes. And he blames me for his failure," she replied in a bitter tone.

"You know," I said suddenly, "I think the first thing I'll do when I get out is cut my hair. You must think that's silly. Something frivolous."

She softened. "No, on the contrary, I understand. It's symbolic. Sometimes we need to cut away certain things to become ourselves. Come on, before we start thinking about our freedom, let's focus on our survival. A nice tall glass of water should do us good."

CHAPTER 10

I HAD WANTED to wait for the right moment to join our secret garden, but I had fallen asleep. Their tranquilizer had really knocked me out.

Golden angel
How you pain me
Sleep, little doll, sleep, sleep
Or I shall die

I woke to the familiar sound of the lullaby, but this time I struggled to fight off sleep. Lulla and Jo were waiting for me at the entrance of our secret hideout, and the moths were fluttering around their heads like magical crowns.

Lulla's mouth was curved in a bewitching smile, while Jo was frowning. I understood her wariness, but after this hellish day, being here with Lulla, my migraine gone, was a moment of respite. No, it was more than that. It was a moment of happiness in the bedlam that my life had become.

The certitude that this place was mine was greater than the fear of what lay within.

So I avoided my friend's sullen gaze to focus on Lulla and this abandoned garden that seemed to be waiting for us.

We laid in the saffrons and she took my hand. We stayed there for a long while, looking up at the pink sunset sky, our fingers intertwined. We didn't know much about each other, yet I felt as if we were bound. Like two twin souls that had found each other at last.

"How long have you been here?" I asked.

"I feel like I've always been here."

"But why? What were you accused of?"

She raised her misshapen hand.

"My parents wanted a different daughter."

Her answer broke my heart. The saddest part was how she said it. As if it were obvious, or normal. As if the only thing that defined her was that hand. She was so much more than that. At Montrose, she was the light in the middle of the darkness, the soft breeze on fragile petals. Candidness and purity incarnated.

I wanted to take her in my arms, but I didn't dare, so I pulled her by the wrist and we ran in the fresh grass, lush as a carpet under our bare feet. I stopped at the marble fountain, placing my hands on the rim to catch my breath. Lulla was laughing.

"Did you see how big and full the moon is?" she asked before spinning in the silvery light.

I plucked a large flower—a chrysanthemum, perhaps—and inhaled its sweet scent.

"This is paradise," I whispered.

She took the flower from me and tucked it behind her ear. "I feel so alive here. Thank you, Hazel, for everything."

"I didn't do anything," I replied, surprised.

She laughed some more and took my hand. Her expression turned grave and she pressed her forehead to mine. "Thank you for being here."

Slowly, her lips closed in on mine. I closed my eyes to savor the moment, the soft caress as light and fleeting as a feather. I wanted the moment to last forever.

But a sharp cry rang out and burst our bubble of bliss.

In front of us, among the ivy and the saffrons, a dark silhouette stood, tall and frightening, a lumbering grotesque man whose face was hidden in the shadows. The little girl was there too. He held her in his sharp claws.

Panic paralyzed me. I couldn't move. I couldn't look away from the girl as she writhed and cried. What should I do? Flee, or try to help her?

But before I could answer the question, Jo grabbed me and Lulla and dragged us toward the exit. The garden seemed to have grown bigger, an endless stretch of ivy, red and green and purple, and thick walls of saffrons. A collision between summer and autumn. A nonsensical jumble.

The girl's cries had ceased and furious steps chased after us. In front of me, Lulla glanced backward, her eyes filled with terror. I didn't dare turn back, too afraid to come face to face with the creature. I had to run, run without stopping to the vanished exit. I saw the horror in Lulla's gaze, and she opened her mouth to speak. To warn. I understood when a sharp pain ran through my skull. Someone had given my braid a rough tug and I toppled backward, falling and rolling to the ground, losing my sense of direction. No matter. My forehead hit against a hard surface and the impact burst in my head, carrying me away into the darkness.

*

When I came to, I was lying in my bed and Jo was patting my face with a damp cloth.

"Don't make a noise," she whispered. "It's still nighttime, and the nurse will make rounds soon. You'll have a nasty bruise on your forehead tomorrow. Say you were searching for your chamber pot in the dark and you hit your head."

I nodded. "And Lulla?" I said with difficulty.

"Don't worry, she's in bed, resting."

She rose in haste. Probably worried not to get caught roaming around in the middle of the night. Once was enough.

I watched her go back to the brightly lit corridor, leaving me in the darkness. What if the creature could come here? What if it could leave the garden? I shuddered at the notion and sat in bed, staring at the light that came from underneath the door. If someone came to my room, I would see them coming.

*

Later, once the fear had passed, I thought about Lulla's lips against mine. A fleeting kiss that almost seemed unreal, a moment of sweetness before horror overtook us, chasing us out of our garden. The verses of my favorite poem came to my mind, and they rang so true now that they sounded almost prophetic.

On my silent lips
I felt the terrifying softness of your first kiss.
Under your feet, I could hear lyres shattering
Crying out to the heavens the proud boredom of poets
In the midst of these languishing moans
Gold of hair you appeared to me.

I took the volume in my hands. It was too dark to read, but no matter. Each word was engraved within me. I didn't know if I would ever see Blanche again, but the loving friendship that had binded us paled in comparison to what I was feeling now. When I saw Lulla, my heart squeezed and butterflies danced in my stomach. When I saw Lulla, I desperately wanted to get out of here and take her with me, far from all the barbarian violence of the hospital. Or, on the contrary, to stay here forever in our autumn garden.

The monster appeared in my mind. What to do?

CHAPTER II

THE NEXT MORNING, Jo was waiting for me well before breakfast.

"We need to talk."

"First I have to see if Lulla is all right."

"After, I promise. But first I really need to talk to you about certain things... That garden. It's too dangerous. We mustn't go back."

"I don't know. The monster is terrifying but... I don't know... I feel like this place is ours, and he has no right to be there. It's like his presence is a sort of profanation."

It was so hard to express my feelings correctly. Was the situation too complex to be explained with simple words, or was I simply struggling to put some order in my thoughts because of the tranquilizers?

"It doesn't matter if he has the right or not. He's there. Nothing about this is normal, and it started when you arrived here."

"You're saying it's my fault?"

"No, of course not. It's not a question of fault. You're not doing this on purpose, but it has something to do with you, I'm sure of it."

"Why?"

"I don't know. Something must have triggered this...gift. Did they give you drugs when you arrived?" I shook my head. "Well, I have no idea then."

"Some of these things... I've seen them before. In my head. And I put them in my stories. The fountain, the violets..."

"So, your imagination is becoming reality?"

I shrugged my shoulder, at a loss. "Wait... I was given bromine."

"Everyone gets bromine here."

I tried to think. Did this strange place have an influence on me? Did it awaken a hidden gift? No, that was absurd. I was an ordinary girl, not a magician. Yet this event had turned my existence around. That, and having my notebook taken away from me.

"Maybe my stories are coming out of my head because I can't write them," I suggested, aware that I was talking nonsense.

"I think we should stay far from this garden. Unless..." She paused to think. "That creature... Why is it there, if it comes from your imagination? Why does it want to harm you?"

"We could enjoy the garden and leave when it arrives."

"Fleeing doesn't solve anything. If it's imaginary, we're not at risk, are we? But you were hurt. I just can't make sense of it. There's no logic to it. My instinct tells me not to go back and maybe we should follow it. Why go looking for answers?"

I touched the bump on my forehead. Unfortunately, the danger did seem real. We had to find a solution. I didn't want the garden to disappear.

"Lulla and I, we're happy there. You know what people will say if they see us together like that in the real world."

"I've been meaning to talk to you about that."

"What?" I asked, suddenly wary. "I hope you're not judging us..."

"You know that's not my style. Be quiet and follow me."

She took me to Lulla's room and pushed the door open. Our friend was lying in bed, her arms against her body, her long fine hair cascading over her shoulders.

"She sleeps a lot. Is it because of her treatments? Are you sure she wasn't wounded last night?"

Jo looked away, ill at ease. "Lulla never woke up from her last session two days ago. The nurses say she's in a coma. It happens sometimes."

"No, that's impossible. She's with us every night."

"She was with us the first night, and you talked to her the next day. The other times, it wasn't her. It wasn't the real Lulla."

"So that wasn't real either? I don't believe you!"

My heart was wilting away, drying out. Soon, there would be nothing left of it but small shreds, swept away by a gust of wind. I looked at the girl lying on her bed, a familiar stranger. A sleeping beauty who would never be kissed awake.

"Are you sure?" I pleaded.

"I wanted to check for myself. Last night, she was already in the garden when I opened the door. And when you were knocked out... She didn't follow us. She can't enter the real world."

"Maybe it's Lulla's soul. Maybe her body is sleeping, but she came with us anyway. I can't abandon her."

"That's one theory. But honestly, she's not the same as the young woman who's locked up here, the one I knew for seven months, who lived her whole life in an asylum and got dozens of rebirth therapies. I think this existence far from a real home broke her. Their insulin shocks destroyed what was left of her."

"I could go every night and destroy the monster. It's the only solution if the Lulla I love doesn't exist in our reality," I stated, determined.

"So you want to stay and rot in this hospital? And end up like Lulla, or even die from one of their little experiments? I don't understand you. I want to get out and fight where I'm needed."

"I don't know what I want," I sobbed.

But I did know. I wanted to see Lulla again. My magical Lulla, born from a lullaby and crowned with butterflies. The one who had kissed me, light as a feather, and made my heart beat.

CHAPTER 12

MY DARLING DOLL
Will not sleep
Close your pretty eyes
Your sapphire eyes
Golden angel
How you pain me
Sleep, little doll, sleep, sleep
Or I shall die

I made my way to the door in the corridor alone. The door that led to my garden of illusions. Dangers be damned, I had to see her again.

"Wait!"

Jo ran to catch up with me.

"What are you doing here?" I snapped.

After our discussion, I had avoided her all day, losing myself in the bland activities that the hospital offered.

"I can't let you go alone. If something happened to you... You're my friend, Hazel Bloom, and what do friends do? They stick together. I think this garden is dangerous and I don't understand why you're compelled to go there, but I want to be there for you."

I saw in her eyes the same determination as when she talked to me about the actions she did with her fellow activists.

"I'll be around, just in case," she added, "but I don't want to come between you and...Lulla."

I understood that it was difficult for her to use that name. We both knew now that it wasn't Lulla Davis. But how else could we call her?

I grasped the handle and pushed the door open. Lulla was waiting for me among the ivy, butterflies fluttering around her. She smiled at me and I hurried toward her.

She was there, and she was real. I took her hand, and it was warm and dense in mine. Something that existed, not just an ethereal dream in the mist. It didn't matter what Jo said, and it didn't matter that my

Lulla wasn't the one who was lying in bed. This was my reality, and no one could take it away. What good was it to look for answers on why and how? The only thing that mattered was the end result: me and her in the garden.

She brushed the tear that was rolling down my cheek and smiled. "Don't be sad," she said simply. "Do you smell the violets? They're blooming for us. Let's get drunk on their scent."

I closed my eyes and breathed in. The fragrance was heady, head-spinning, more than it should be. Stronger, because none of this was real. Lulla seemed to read my mind. She looked at me the way a mother looked at her pouting child and took a step back. A butterfly landed on the tip of my nose and I laughed in spite of myself. A mix of amused giggles and exhausted sobs.

"Here, you are queen," she said. "That creature... It has no right to impose its rule. You must master it."

Easy to say. How to master a feral beast?

"This garden, whatever happens, will never disappear. It'll always be here," she said, tapping my temple. "Now, Hazel Bloom, what do you want?"

I wanted to forget the girl in the coma. The hospital.

She pulled on my arm and asked me to help her pick flowers and ivy.

"Crowns, that's what we need. Have you ever made flower crowns? Recite one of your pretty poems while I take care of it."

"*I was trembling. Long blessed lilies of white were dying in your hands like cold candles. Their passing scent escaped your fingers, a breath of supreme anguish. From your pale clothes exhaled agony and love, one after the other.*"

She gave an ecstatic sigh and put her creation on my head, a crown of violets, saffrons, and busy lizzies. Flowers that never bloom at the same time in the real world.

"Did you ever think about what you'd do once you were outside?" I whispered.

A useless question. How can you ask someone in a coma how she imagines her future? Or a young woman born of dreams? There was no future possible.

"Outside? I don't want to go back to my parents. We're happy here."

"Yes, you're right," I answered, not knowing whether her answer was hers or mine. Did she have a will of her own, or were her words only the reflection of my own buried thoughts?

She leaned toward me and kissed me. Her lips were soft against mine. She smelled like violets and soil. The scent of the garden. A girl born from the flowers.

"Come on, Hazel," interrupted Jo. "It's time to go back. Before the monster comes. Perhaps you should say your goodbyes. You decide."

I could tell by her gaze that she was struggling not to order me. I followed her halfheartedly, glancing behind me at Lulla. She stayed in our wake, a few steps behind, and gave me a trusting smile whenever my eyes landed on her.

Jo opened the door and I lingered for a few moments, not wanting to close it. Taking my fill of the bewitching sight of Lulla amid the flowers and the butterflies.

How could I give any of this up? It was impossible.

CHAPTER 13

AWKWARDNESS HAD INSTILLED itself between Jo and me, a cold, tense distance. I wanted to save my garden and see Lulla again. She wanted me to turn my back on them and face reality.

We pretended to be busy with our various daily activities: the overcooked eggs, the splotches of colors on the canvas, the Bible verses. All of which we did under Bertha's watchful eye that brimmed with satisfaction at our docility. Free time was the trickiest moment. What was left unsaid weighed down on us, urging us to speak.

Finally, I sat down next to her. She was still my friend. I knew she wanted the best for me. She thought she was doing what was right.

"Listen, Jo—"

"Mrs. Foley, your husband has come to visit," Mabel interrupted us.

Jo blinked. For the first time, I saw a hint of fear in her eyes. She rose and followed the nurse to a far table where a tall blond man was seated. She took a seat in front of him. I strained my ear to hear them, but I couldn't make out a word they were saying. However, I could tell their discussion was most serious. Jo was tense, and she even hit her fist against the table, while her husband stayed relaxed in his chair. Then I saw tears of rage and despair in my friend's eyes, two pools of helplessness faced with injustice.

"You had no right to sell that house!" she cried out. "It's been in my family for generations! It's all I have left of my parents!"

I ran toward them, sensing what would happen next.

"You don't own anything. It's all mine now. Even the dress on your back, that I was generous enough to provide," the odious man snapped.

The slap of flesh against flesh rang out like a rifle shot. The nurses leaped toward Jo, needle in hand.

"Stop it!" I exclaimed.

I was unable to do anything else. Bertha wrapped her arms around my waist, holding me back, while Jo kicked and screamed, biting the arms that came at her. The needle finally found its mark in her shoulder and her body went limp like a ragdoll.

"Why?" I murmured to myself.

Bertha had heard me. She sniggered. "We're not going to let loonies make a spectacle of themselves. A hefty dose of bromine, nothing like it to stop hysterical fits."

"Her condition is getting worse," her husband remarked calmly. "I fear I must insist on a more aggressive treatment. I wish to see Doctor Pierce."

"Right away, sir."

I wanted to spit in his face. He knew. He knew that when he told Josephine about selling the house, he would make her lose her temper. All of it was a vile strategy to make sure she would stay locked up forever in Montrose Asylum.

I tried to hold back the tears that were rising to my eyes. He had just robbed her of her only chance at a normal life, a life where she could live according to her values. She only had two choices left: go back and play the perfect wife with her terrible husband, or stay in an insane asylum.

Bertha let me go to follow the group of nurses who were taking my friend away, giving me one last warning look.

If I tried anything funny, I would get a massive dose of bromine, or worse.

Time passed and Jo didn't come back. What would they do to her? Maybe she'd get the same treatment as Lulla Davis. Or another hydrotherapy session. I couldn't help a horrified shudder and sobs tore at my chest.

I spent the entire day on the lookout, trying to pick up information, trying to overhear anything the nurses told each other, but my so-called disinterested air didn't fool anyone, and I was too anxious to look innocent. I simply managed to glean unpleasant looks. I wasn't as skilled as Josephine in that respect.

"If you don't calm down," Mabel told me, "I'm going to ask that they increase your dose of bromine."

I tried to smile to reassure her. I still remembered the migraine and the foggy state I'd been in after taking that hefty dose of tranquilizer. Thankfully, Mabel wasn't Bertha, and she let me leave without following through with her threat.

*

Night came. I was lying in bed, too distressed to fall asleep, waiting for the lullaby that would lead me to the garden. Maybe I could find some relief there. Yet it wasn't the child's crystalline voice that resounded through the corridor, but the creaking of a wheelchair.

I slipped out of bed and cracked the door open. Bertha was taking Jo back to her room. I waited for her to leave and joined my friend.

"Jo, I was so worried! I hope they didn't give you the same treatment as Lulla."

Jo was seated in her wheelchair and didn't move. I took a step toward her, making out her face in the dimness.

"Jo..."

I knelt before her and placed my hand over hers. It was warm, but strangely inert. I switched on the lamp on the nightstand.

The feeble light sent shadows against the wall and it took me a few seconds to understand what I was seeing.

Jo's gaze was dulled, empty. Her face seemed strangely doughy. And her head... They'd shaved off a part of her hair and coarse black stitches closed a scalpel wound. They had opened her skull, maybe even her brain... For what? To cure here? No, to silence her. I lay my head on her knees and wept.

My dear, impetuous friend. To see her reduced to a living corpse broke my heart and gripped my throat. This place was destroying us, breaking our spirit and leaving us to die.

My only hope was that her state was only temporary, a side effect of the operation, and that tomorrow, she would be the same as I'd known her.

CHAPTER 14

MY DARLING DOLL
  Will not sleep
  Close your pretty eyes
  Your sapphire eyes
  Golden angel
  How you pain me
  Sleep, little doll, sleep, sleep
  Or I shall die

I had fallen asleep on the floor in a sitting position, my head on my friend's knees. I rose, my limbs stiff and aching, and shuffled to the door from where the lullaby came.

Lulla was waiting for me, her arms wide open, as if she was aware of my torment. Which was only logical, since she was a product of my imagination. A part of myself. I leaned into her embrace, thinking of Jo in her wheelchair and the real Lulla in her bed. Stolen, broken lives.

Lulla was wearing a crown of green ivy. After she had held me in her arms, she took it off to place it on my head.

We walked in silence across the meadow of violets. I was like a sleepwalker, a prisoner of my dreams and nightmares.

The greenery started to shiver, and the flowers shrank beneath my feet.

I was the queen, my friend had told me. So I wouldn't flee. This masquerade had lasted only too long. Maybe my crown would magically endow me with strength and courage.

The dark silhouette moved forward. It was only a man, a tall one, but not the misshapen monster I had thought I'd seen the first time.

"Who are you and what do you want?" I asked, lifting my chin and trying to adopt Jo's reckless tone.

A grunt, or maybe a laugh, resounded and the man stepped into the light. I thought I would see his face, but it was hidden by a wooden mask. I couldn't see the details from this distance and I didn't know what to do. Approach him? Fight him? Interrogate him? Could he even speak? Perhaps fleeing wasn't such a bad idea after all.

Fear paralyzed me and numbed my brain. I glanced at Lulla, hoping for a gesture, a sign.

"The garden, him, me, we're all linked," she told me.

"What does that mean?"

"I can't leave this place, but he can't either."

"I don't understand," I sobbed.

Lulla said nothing. I couldn't grasp what she was trying to make me understand, but I must have known the answer. If Lulla came from my imagination, it meant I had everything in hand to fight. Her knowledge was mine.

The man had drawn closer and didn't wait for me to make a decision. He slowly brought his hand to my throat and squeezed. And squeezed.

Pain. No air.

Could he kill me? Could I die here? A small part of me wanted to give up, to sink into nothingness, yearning for oblivion.

But just as I was about to give in to this impulse, Lulla launched herself at the man, wrapping her arms around his neck and her legs around his torso. The man let me go to get rid of his assailant.

"Don't worry about me!" she cried. "Run! He can't hurt me, only you can! You are queen here, don't forget it!"

I hesitated a moment, then whipped around and ran along the corridor, to the exit, and the real world.

CHAPTER 15

I GOT UP before breakfast to go to Jo's room. She was still in the same position, her gaze lost in the void.

"Josephine? Can you hear me? It's me, Hazel."

She didn't flinch. Her face stayed expressionless. Was her spirit even still there? Was it trapped in a corner of her mind? Maybe she could hear but couldn't answer. Unless she was gone altogether. Vanished. Dead.

I dragged myself down to the dining room. I, too, felt dead inside. Then I pictured Jo's furious expression. No, I couldn't wallow in self-pity. My friends had been robbed of their freedom to choose, but I could still choose my destiny. In such a place, choices were limited, but there was still hope. I had to cling to it. For Jo. For Lulla.

I sat at a table. Gloria was already starting to fill her pockets with food. Ann swayed back and forth, lost in her own world. Charlotte rubbed at a spot on her glass. We were all trapped in a bubble, prisoners of our own demons. It would be so easy to let go, to give in to fear and despair. To live only for my nightly escapades. A few minutes, a few hours of reprieve from the horror of this place. Or even to give myself to the creature in the garden.

But I couldn't do that to Josephine, or to the real Lulla. I had to fight because they couldn't any longer. Maybe I would end up like them, but at least I would have tried to live, to get out of here.

I felt like a dandelion blowing in the wind, ready to be blown apart and scattered at the slightest breeze. I had to become a reed, plying in the gales to stand up again. Tonight, I would face the monster. Face my fears. And say goodbye to my dear Lulla...

How sweet it had been to let myself be lulled by illusions. Alas, it had to come to an end.

*

"You seem preoccupied," Doctor Bromfield said. "I was told Josephine Foley was your friend."

"Yes, she's my friend." I sighed before continuing. "I thought I was ready to face my fears... The monster inside my mind..."

"A remarkable metaphor. And the fact that you're admitting to this is a huge step forward on the path to healing."

I nodded, holding back tears. He had no idea. "I know I hold the keys."

"You're right. Oftentimes, patients don't understand that they are the instrument of their own recovery. My role is to guide you."

"Yes."

"However, you seem tense. Emotional. Maybe all of this is too much for you. You have to take it one step at a time. Maybe I should increase your doses of bromine. I'd ask my colleague, but I fear he'll simply take matters into his own hands. We don't exactly see eye to eye when it comes to therapy. He prefers the scientific way, whereas I favor psychoanalysis."

I straightened. I didn't want more tranquilizers. I wanted to be in full possession of my means to go back to the garden.

"Everything is fine, I assure you. The scene I witnessed was a bit...violent. You know, with Josephine. But it makes me want to recover even more."

"I understand. Don't hesitate to tell me if you feel overwhelmed by your emotions. That's what I'm here for. To listen to you, but also to prescribe medicine. It can help, provide support."

Support that gave me a migraine and numbed my brain. I nodded nonetheless to look like I agreed with him.

CHAPTER 16

MY DARLING DOLL
  Will not sleep
  Close your pretty eyes
  Your sapphire eyes
  Golden angel
  How you pain me
  Sleep, little doll, sleep, sleep
  Or I shall die

Alone in the corridor, I followed the voice. I thought about what Jo had told me, but also what Doctor Bromfield had said. I had to face my fears. Expose them to the light. I pushed the door open. Lulla was waiting for me. She took my hand and whispered in my ear.

"You can do it. You can kill the monster."

"If I do that, the garden will disappear... And so will you..."

"Shhh. I know. It doesn't matter."

Her lips brushed against mine, soft and warm, then she stepped back, tilting her head. Our last kiss tasted like wilted flowers and a goodbye. I had to go on without her. This was my struggle, not hers.

Ivy rustled and butterflies fluttered around me as I moved on. The still tranquility of the garden had given way to distressed agitation. I saw the little girl in the distance, but she ran away, swallowed by the darkness.

As I walked, the green leaves turned to shades of gold and copper, and by the time I reached the marble fountain, they were a bright shade of crimson. I went ahead, further than I'd ever gone before. A dark, disturbing silhouette stood in the wilderness.

He was there in front of me, and this time I wouldn't flee. He stepped out of the shadow that cloaked his face. He was a tall, dark-haired man whose face was hidden by a wooden mask that brought to mind the pagan gods of ancient tales.

I took a step forward and held out my hand to tear off this grotesque disguise, to see at last whom I was facing. To know who the monster was that haunted my mind.

I plunged my eyes into his dark gaze and fell. And fell. And fell. Ever faster, ever deeper, with no end. I closed my eyes.

I was four years old. I was playing in the garden, it was springtime, and I was picking a bouquet of violets.

"Tell me, my little doll, would you wish to marry me?" Uncle George asked.

"No," I laughed. "You're a boy. Boys are ugly. I'm going to marry Clare. She's got shiny soft red hair."

I was four years old. The air was warm, but the sun was sinking behind the ivy-covered wall.

"Come here, my little doll, so I can sing you a song."

My darling doll
Will not sleep
Close your pretty eyes
Your sapphire eyes
Golden angel
How you pain me
Sleep, little doll, sleep, sleep
Or I shall die

I didn't like Uncle George's voice. I sat on the bench beside him, hoping he'd stop. He placed a hand on my knee. Slid further up my thigh. I didn't like that at all. Not his raspy skin against mine, nor his breath that smelled of tobacco.

I was four years old. Dusk was already falling on the garden. The ivy had turned red, like the squirrels. Uncle George sat beside me, humming.

"Be a good girl, my little doll."

As usual, I didn't feel anything. No sound, no smell, no sensation. I focused on the purple flowers that swayed in the breeze. On the tree trunk. If I stared long enough, a face appeared in its creases. On the moth that fluttered by, landed on my arm, then took off again. On the cracked marble fountain Mother wanted to have destroyed.

When he was done, he leaned over me and whispered, "Don't forget, not a word about this! If you tell anyone, I'll say that you're lying. See those flowers? They're saffrons. Just a few seeds are enough to prepare a mortal poison. You wouldn't want something to happen to your parents, would you? But if something did happen to them, you wouldn't have to worry. I'd become your tutor. I'll take care of you."

I hit the ground hard and curled up, overwhelmed with the emotions churning inside of me. Fear, horror, pain, despair, anger. Then I heard a voice. The little girl was standing there, crying. I looked up and she ran off. I stood up.

"Wait! Come back!"

That girl. It was me. Me at four years old. I caught her and took her in my arms. I was in so much pain. I could have cowered in a corner and waited for death to free me of these awful memories. But I couldn't leave this little girl here, alone and lost. I stroked her hair and murmured words of comfort. I wanted to rock her to sleep, but the only lullaby that came to my head was that wretched song. So I hummed the verses of my book.

The languid night no longer fears the sun
Enveloping it in veils of otherworldly blue
Extinguishing the far away light of the stars
And poppy wine will pour a measure of sleep.

Little by little, she faded away. Pale and transparent. Unreal. And the garden itself was vanishing. The ivy was shrinking to reveal the gray wall of the hospital, and Lulla stood there, her lips curved into a sad smile. I wanted to run to her, but my body was heavy. I felt as if I was moving in slow motion along the corridor and its fading colors. When I reached her at last, she was nothing more than a fleeting, evanescent dream, and I was alone in the abandoned corridor.

CHAPTER 17

I HAD DEFEATED the monster. Had I defeated my fears? I wasn't so certain. My memories weighed heavily on my heart, a burden that would stay with me my whole life. I felt dirty, broken, incomplete. As if he had stolen something from me in that garden—the garden I had forgotten about, that Mother had remodeled when I was six.

However, I also felt as if a part of me had stayed trapped in the magical place my own imagination had created, and that this small part of my soul had come back to me.

I simply had to figure out how to live with it. I was like a broken piece of china that had be put back together, without knowing if all the pieces were there, or how to make them fit together.

I also had to honor the memory of Jo and Lulla—the real Lulla, who was forever asleep, and the Lulla of my dreams, who was forever gone. I had to be strong and get out of here. I had to live.

I went back to my room, tears streaming down my face, torn between all those contrary feelings. I was about to open the door when a voice boomed out. Bertha's voice.

"Well, look who it is, wandering the halls at night. And in what state! You've been awfully fidgety these past two days. Is the bromine no longer working?"

I opened my mouth to answer, but the needle was already in my arm under the smug glare of the nurse.

A black blur took me under.

*

I tried to open my eyelids, but they were so heavy... Who had put stones over them? Why was I reeling? I felt like I was being tossed around by an angry sea.

"Insulin, please," a masculine voice said.

Darkness again.

*

When I woke, I was drenched in sweat, my whole body burning while the surface of my skin was freezing.

"Oh! My baby woke up!"

A big-breasted nurse took me in her arms and started rocking me slowly. My teeth were chattering.

"Shhhh... Everything is fine, my little angel."

She kissed my forehead. The colors were so bright. I felt like I was about to throw up.

"Wait here, I'll get a bottle with sugared water for you."

The nurse stood up, softly laying my head back on the pillow. The room seemed to spin around me like a crazed carousel. I closed my eyes to lessen the sensation, but with little success. Nausea and vertigo still whirled within me, waltzing like two desperate lovers.

So that was their rebirth? It was more like dying. I was about to push the nurse and her ridiculous bottle away when my muscles contracted violently. Pain racked through my body as I was overtaken with spasms. I didn't understand what was happening. A hot stream flowed under me as blackness crept on the edge of my vision.

"Doctor! Hurry! She's convulsing!"

Steps hurried closer. I plunged into the abyss.

*

When I had woken up several hours before, I had the sensation of returning from the dead. A resurrection? Maybe, but not the one promised by the doctors with their insulin and the motherly nurses. I had come back from Hell itself, broken but somehow stronger.

I was going to hold my promise.

I smiled demurely at Doctor Pierce, who showered me with praise. He had come to see me every day this week to assess my state.

"Our insulin shock had never worked so well. It's wonderful. I'm going to write a report and send it to the *Journal of Nervous and Mental Diseases*. Contact Doctor Sakel, even. Your therapy will continue with Bromfield."

Good. I knew what to tell him... Not the truth, for I already knew, in my situation, that women or even children would never prevail. We were nothing but inferior beings with fragile, perverted minds. Insignificant creatures.

No matter. I already had a plan. I was going to get out of here, put my life back in order, and fulfill my dreams. And Jo's as well.

CHAPTER 18

Six months later

I was strangely calm. I was about to do the single most terrible act of justice there was, and no warring feelings fought within me. Like the dark, still waters of Greenwood Lake, undisturbed by the slightest breeze.

Serenity. That was the best word for it. I stood in front of the lovely opulent house that was no doubt shaded by the tall leafy trees when summer came around. A beautiful setting that kept it hidden from view. But in February, the branches looked more like skeletal arms scratching in accusation at the windows.

I stepped onto the pavement. On my right, a gate creaked open and I turned my head. A young woman had just left her house and was walking down the street, her back to me. But I had caught a glimpse of her. His neighbor was pregnant. This only strengthened my determination.

Another step. And another. The wrought-iron gate was perfectly oiled and opened without a sound. I didn't head to the front door, but walked around the house and slipped toward the back door. It wasn't locked and I pushed it open, stepping directly into the kitchen.

A cup of tea was brewing on the table. I didn't have much time. I took the vial out of my pocket. Ten seeds was enough to kill a man. I used twenty. I poured the powder in the dark tea and hid inside the pantry as I heard footsteps approaching.

I hadn't closed the door completely so as not to make any noise, but also to enjoy the view. But he only took the cup and left the room again. I had to follow him in silence, make sure he didn't notice me. Not now, at least. Thankfully, the monster was noisy, and even if I couldn't see him, I could guess what he was doing.

Heavy steps. Heavy steps. The clink of china against wood. The rustling of paper. I crept toward his study and glimpsed inside through the crack in the door.

He was sorting through files. He raked a hand through his hair, then took the cup and drank a sip. He grimaced and drank some more.

I opened the door and he looked up from his work. His eyes widened with shock. My still waters remained undisturbed as I drew closer to my goal.

"What are you doing here?" he stammered.

His hands were trembling. I wish I could say he was afraid of me, but no. Not yet. It was just the poison doing its job.

"Hello, Uncle George. I came to deliver a message."

His face fell. He was struggling to breathe. Good. Very good.

"I'm not some delicate poppy that you can pluck from the ground, quick to wilt away... A flower you can crush in your fist. I am the saffron that wraps its roots around your neck."

I opened my hand to reveal a purple saffron. A flower in bloom, as if I'd just picked it.

"How is that poss—"

His words were lost in a strangled gurgle. I laughed joylessly.

"You're dying, and that's all you have to say?! I don't understand your question. How is it possible that I left the asylum where you had me committed? That a lamb can turn into a wolf? Or that I found a saffron in the middle of winter?"

I contemplated my work for a moment, then answered. "It's always fall in my inner garden. An agonizing nature... The place in which you imprisoned me so many years ago. But now I'm free."

He fell from his chair, seized by convulsions. I could only see his foot lurching on the floor. Then it stopped. It was all over.

"I'm not the monster in this family."

I didn't feel a hint of satisfaction or regret. I had done my duty. No other girl would be a victim of his perversity. I had killed a man, but how many more people had I saved?

I left his house. The street was deserted. Two addresses awaited in my pocket. One was a publishing house, the other Margaret Sanger. I wasn't naive enough to believe we would change things, but I hoped to sow the seeds of justice, so that our daughters and their daughters could bear witness to a new, better world. A world where they would be heard.

I am the tender and terrible Mistress.

For I possess the art of wonderful poisons,

Insinuating and sweet as treachery

And more voluptuous than the eloquent lie.

Renée Vivien, « Locusta »

NOTES

THE SAKEL CURE, named after the psychiatrist Manfred Sakel (1900-1957), also called insulin shock or insulin therapy, was invented in 1927 and used until the 1960s. It was supposed to cure schizophrenia but also psychopathy, drug dependency, catatonia, severe depression, and mania. It was a dangerous, ineffective method, like many treatments at the time.

Officially, the practice of lobotomy started in 1935, but it existed before. The first brain surgery to cure mental illness was done in 1888.

If this topic interests you, here are the books that helped me when I wrote this novel:

The Female Malady, by Elaine Showalter

Women of the Asylum, by Jeffrey L. Geller and Maxine Harris

One last word about the ending. I really wish it could have been different, that Hazel could have told her story to her therapist and then the police, but in the 1920s, such a thing was impossible. Victims were considered liars, told that hysteria gave them too much imagination, or purely and simply demonized. Their persecutors became the victims of female seduction (or even seduction by children!), especially if they were wealthy and respectable. At the time, those who tried to obtain justice paid a heavy price.

This topic is studied at length in the following book: *Redefining Rape: Sexual Violence in the Era of Suffrage and Segregation,* by Estelle B. Freedman (Harvard University Press).

About the Author

Cécile Guillot is a French award winner author who published a dozen novels, mostly dark contemporary fantasy, gothic and horror books.